P9-ARG-285

eton woke up.

hic,
hic,
hic

To Kiko

—M. C.

To Susan—my online savvy shopper who found me the best bones

—S. D. S.

ALADDIN PAPERBACKS
An imprint of Simon & Schuster Children's Publishing Division
1230 Avenue of the Americas, New York, NY 10020

Also available in a Margaret K. McElderry Books hardcover edition.
Designed by Kristin Smith
The text of this book was set in Caxton.
The illustrations were rendered in gouache, watercolor, and ink.
Manufactured in China
First Aladdin Paperbacks edition August 2005
10 9 8 7 6 5 4 3 2 1
The Library of Congress has cataloged the hardcover edition as follows:
Cuyler, Margery
Skeleton hiccups / Margery Cuyler ; illustrated by S. D. Schindler.—1st ed.
p. cm.
Summary: Ghost tries to help Skeleton get rid of the hiccups.
ISBN 0-689-84770-X (hc.)
[1. Hiccups—Fiction. 2. Ghosts—Fiction. 3. Skeleton—Fiction.] I. Schindler, S. D., ill. II. Title.
PZ7.C997 Sk 2002 [E]—dc21 2001044121 ISBN 1-4169-0276-7 (Aladdin pbk.)

SkeLeTON hiCcups

by margery cuyler

illustrated by s. d. schindler

Aladdin Paperbacks

New York London Toro

Had the hiccups.
hic, hic, hic

hic,
hic,
hic

Took a shower.

Brushed his teeth.

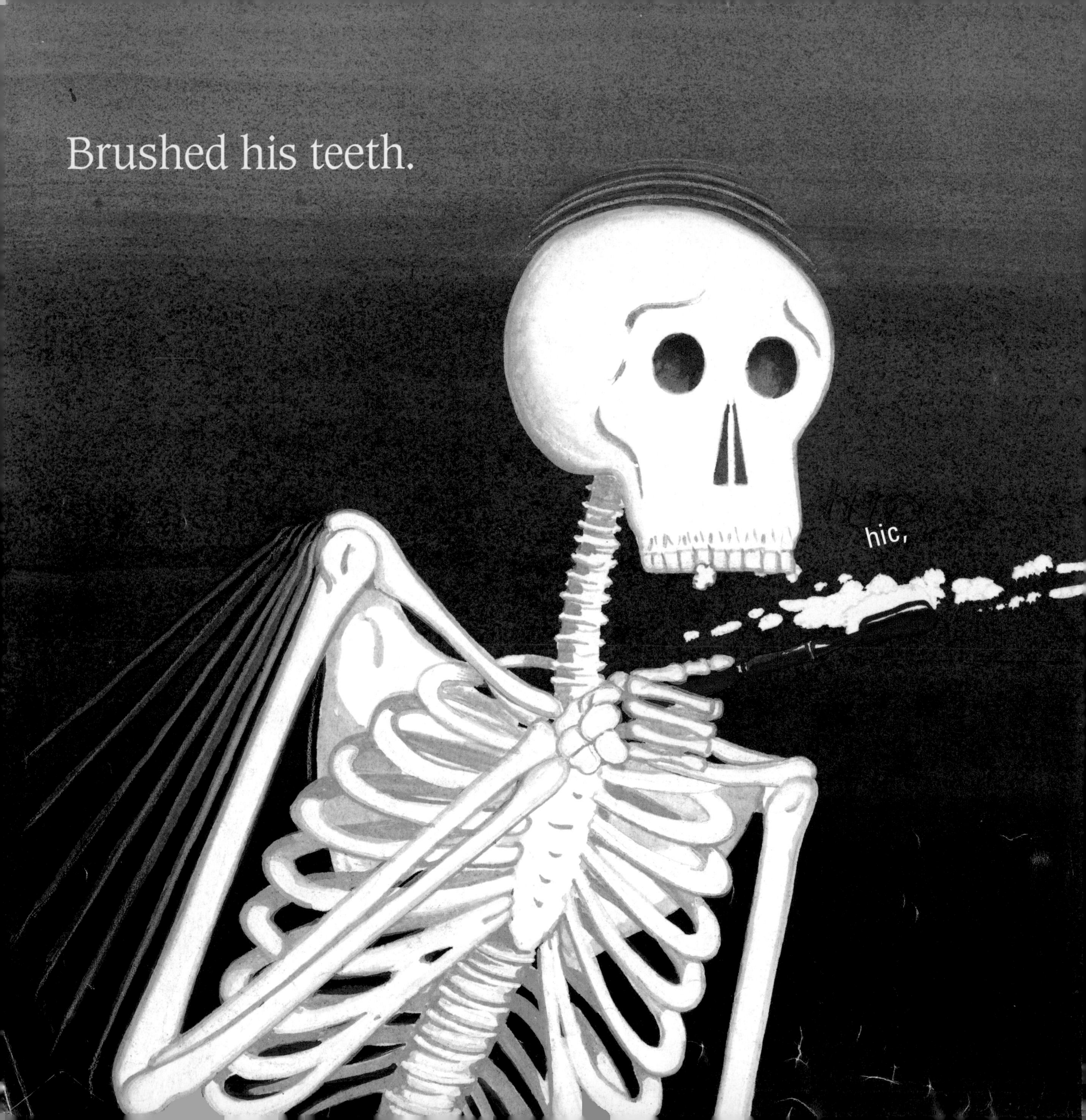

hic,
hic

Ghost-White
BONE
POLISH

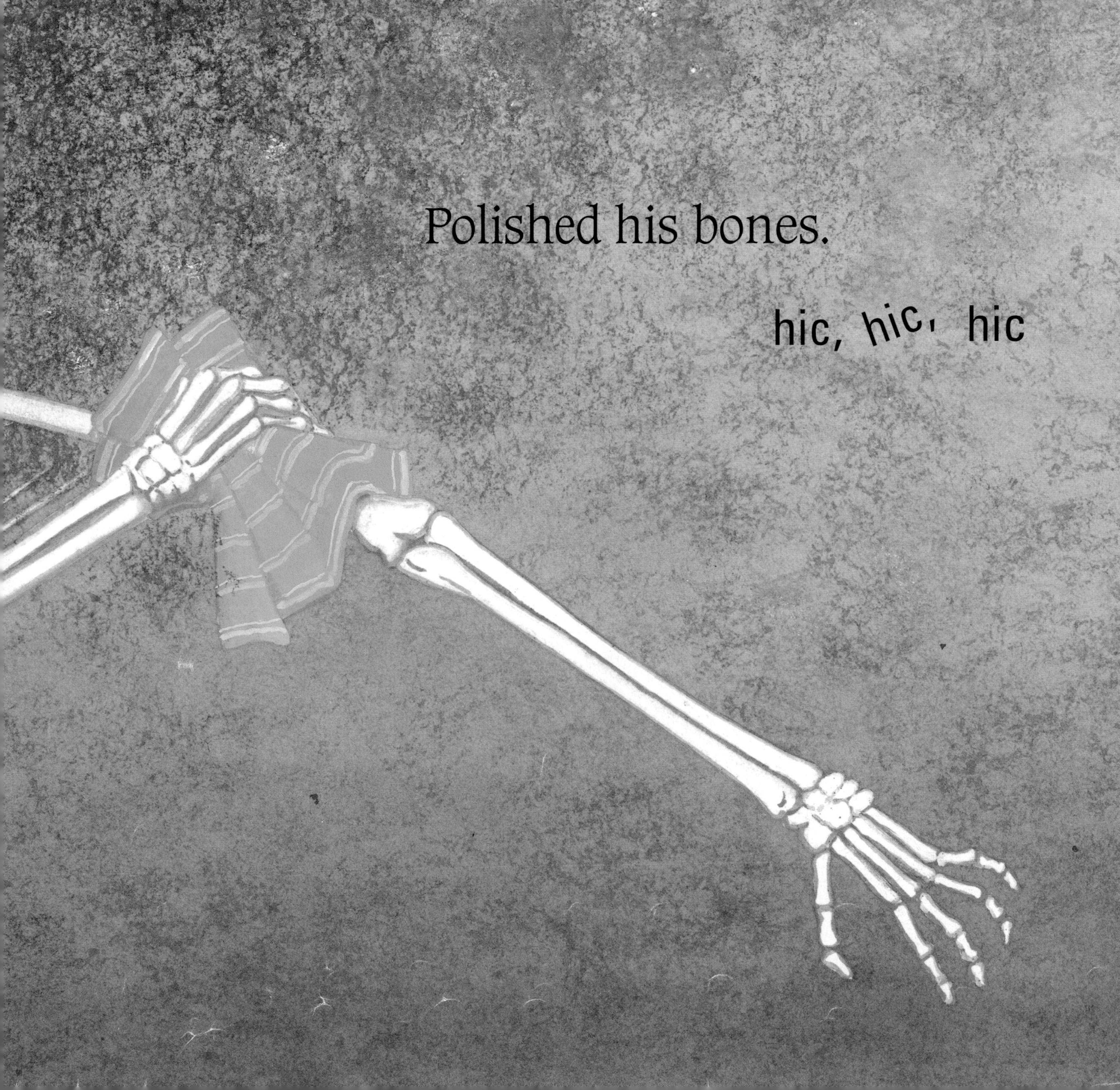

Polished his bones.

hic, hic, hic

Carved a pumpkin.

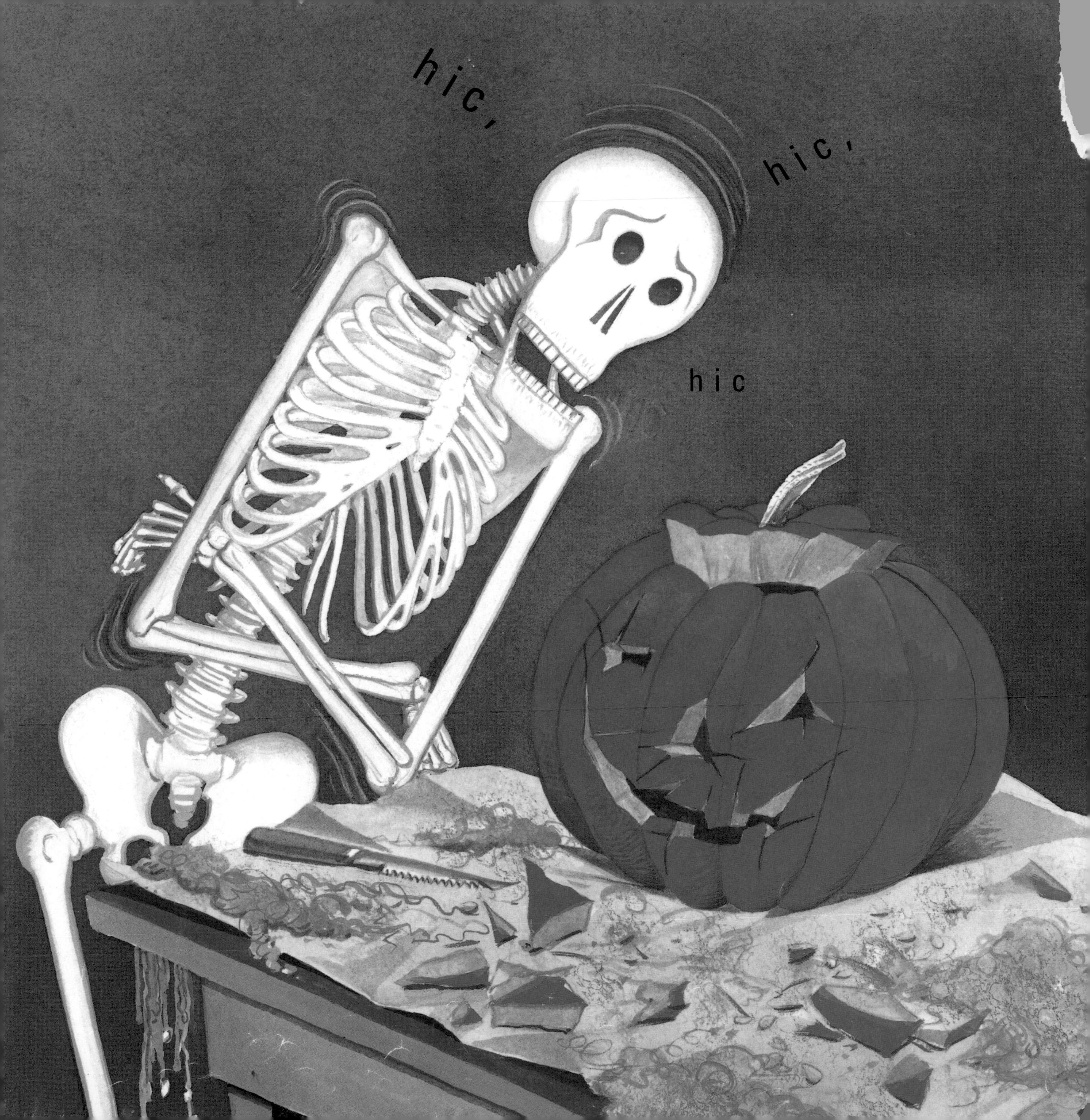
hic,
hic,
hic

Raked some leaves.

Played with Ghost.

Ghost told Skeleton,

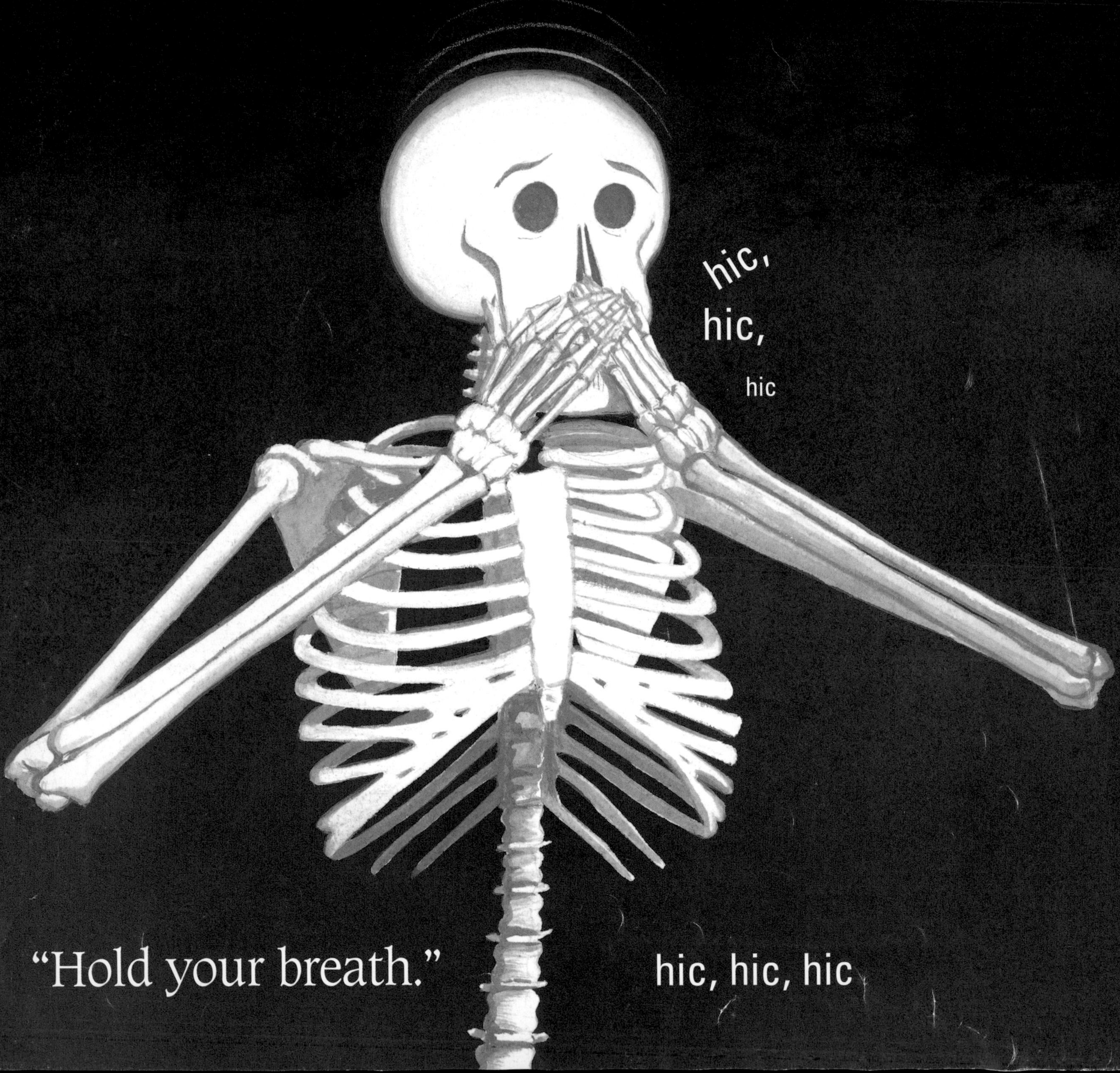

hic,
hic,
hic

"Hold your breath."

hic, hic, hic

“Eat some sugar.”

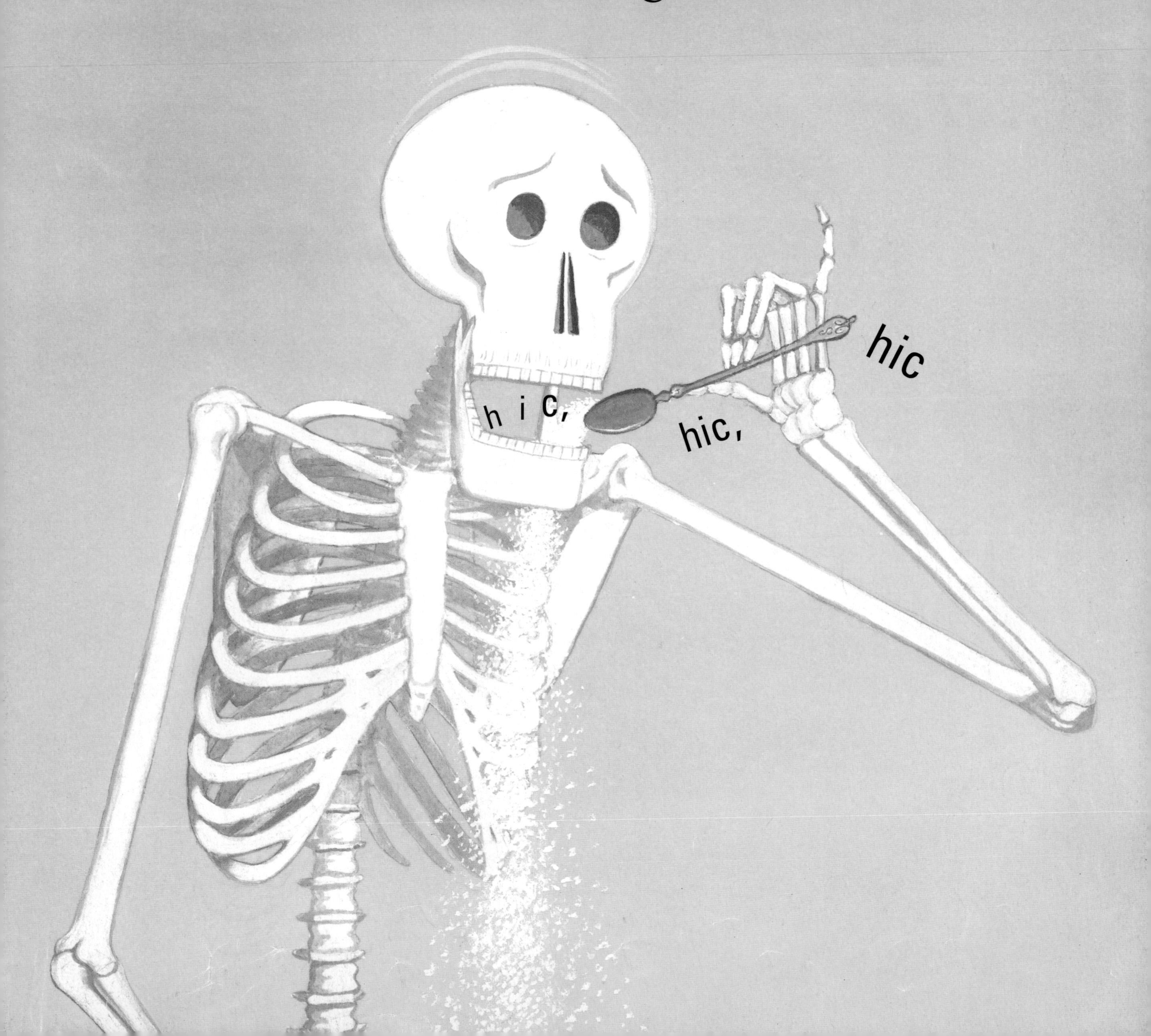

"Press your fingers . . .

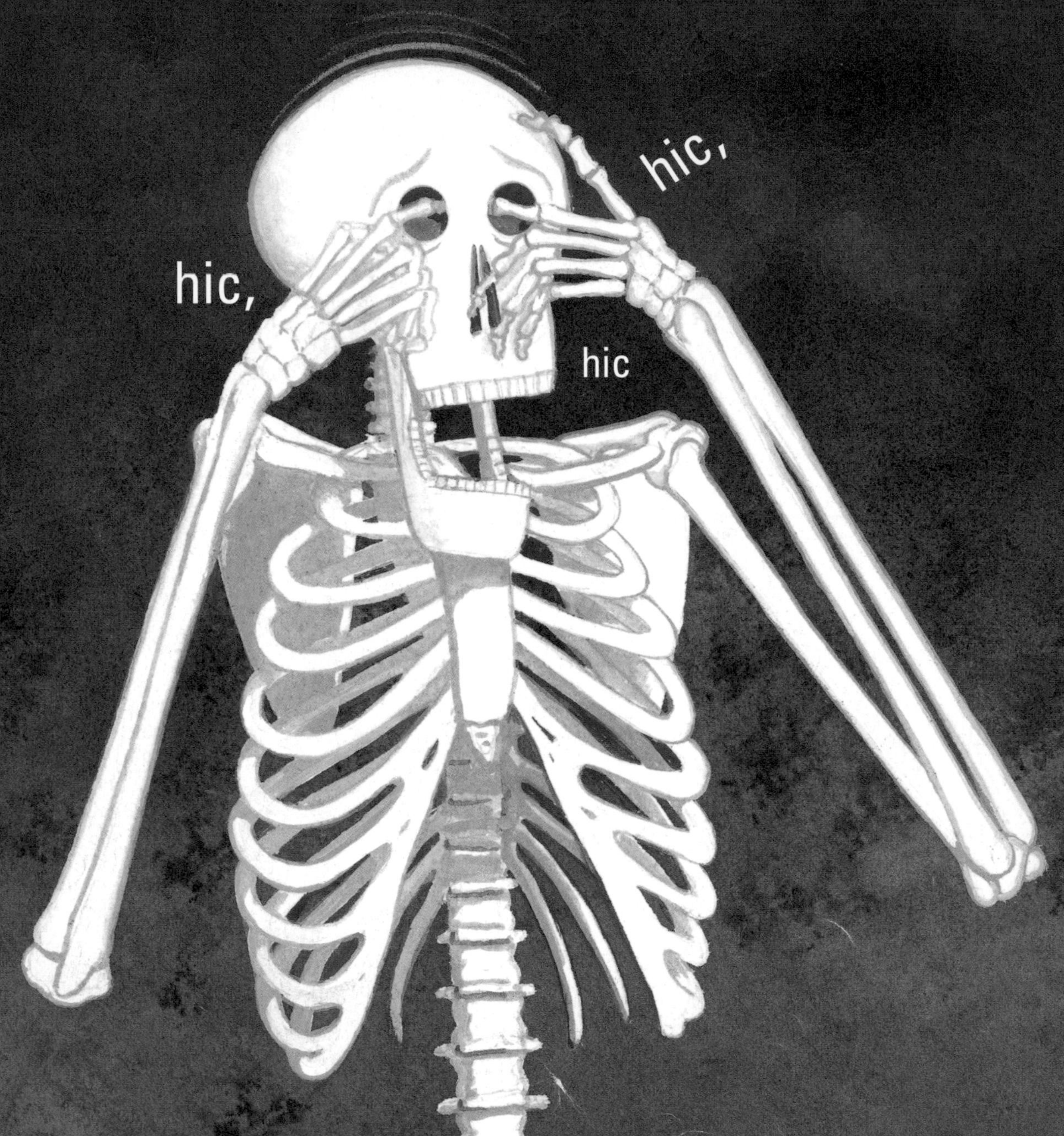

over your eyeballs."

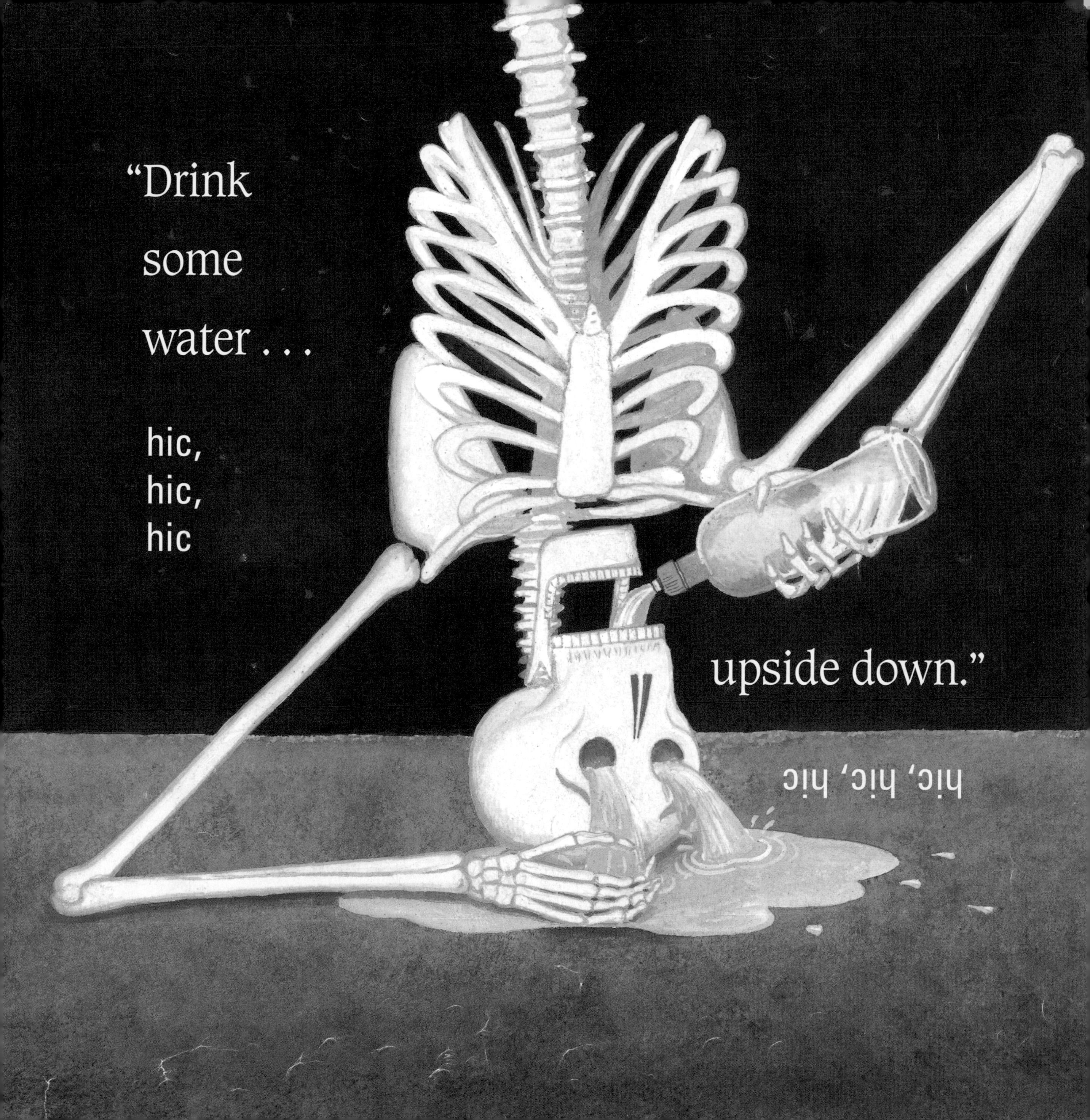
"Drink
some
water . . .
hic,
hic,
hic
upside down."
hic, hic, hic

Ghost made a face.

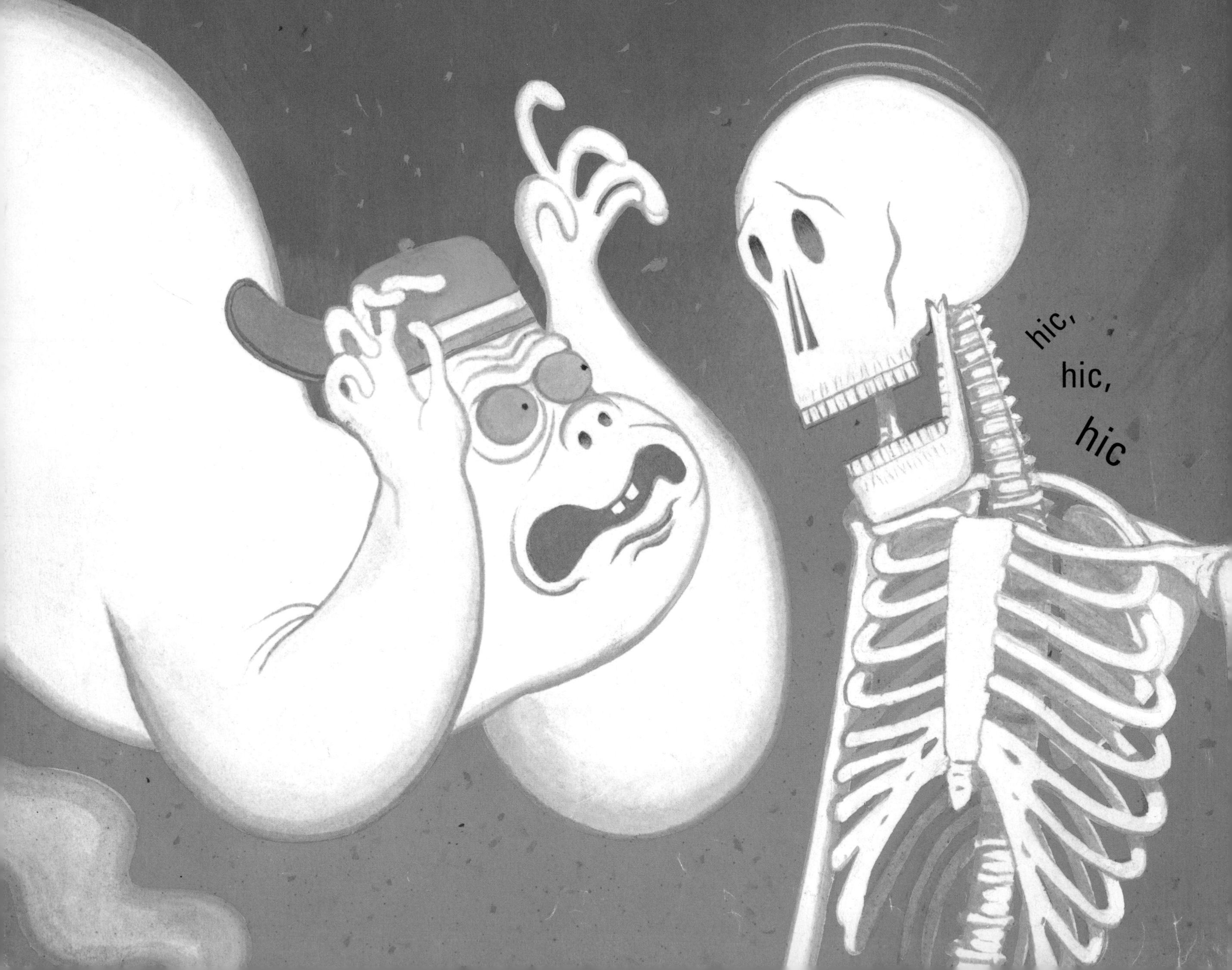

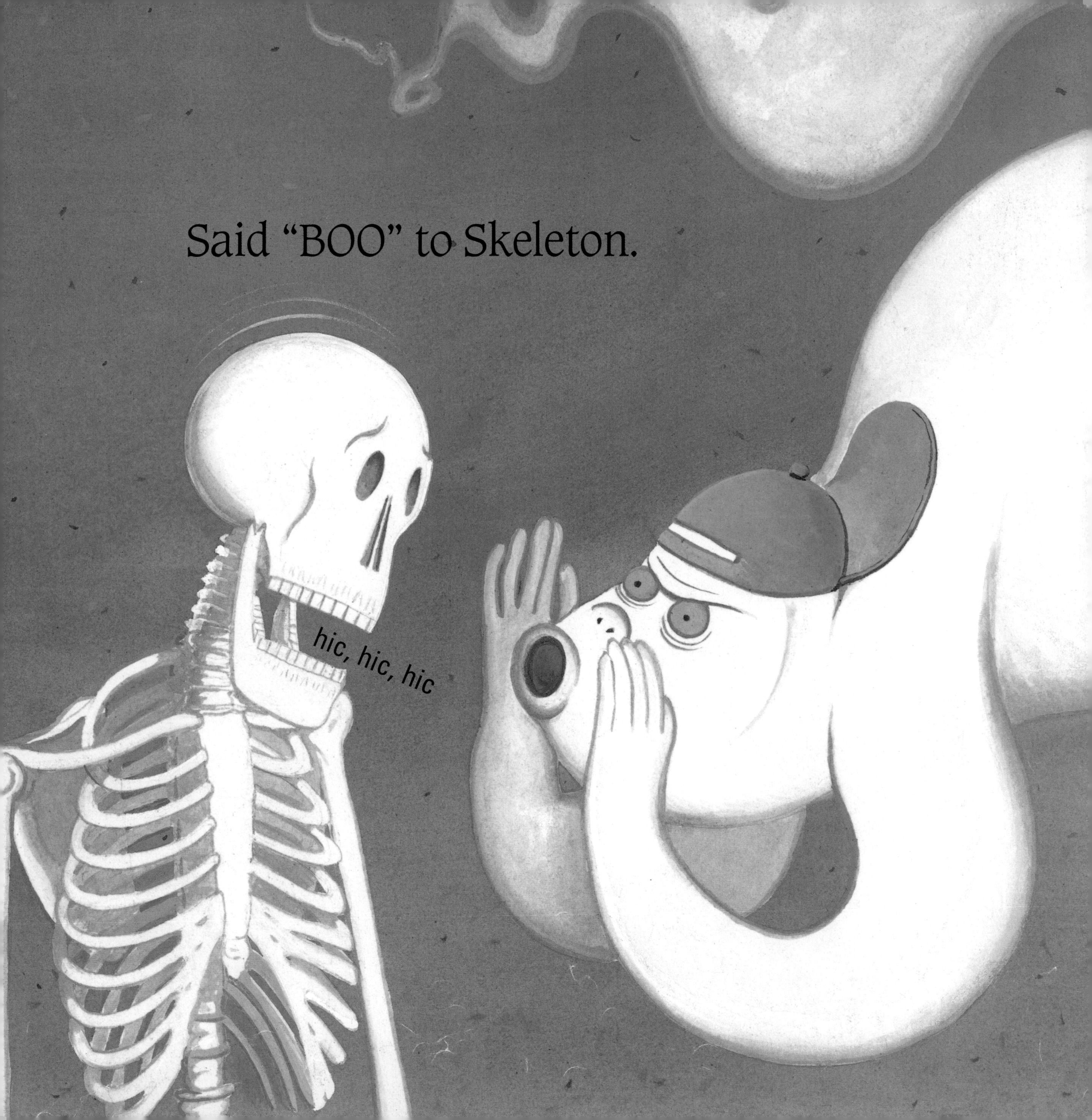

Said "BOO" to Skeleton.

But nothing worked.
hic, hic, hic
The hiccups stayed.
hic,
hic,
hic

Then Ghost got smart.

hic, hic, hic

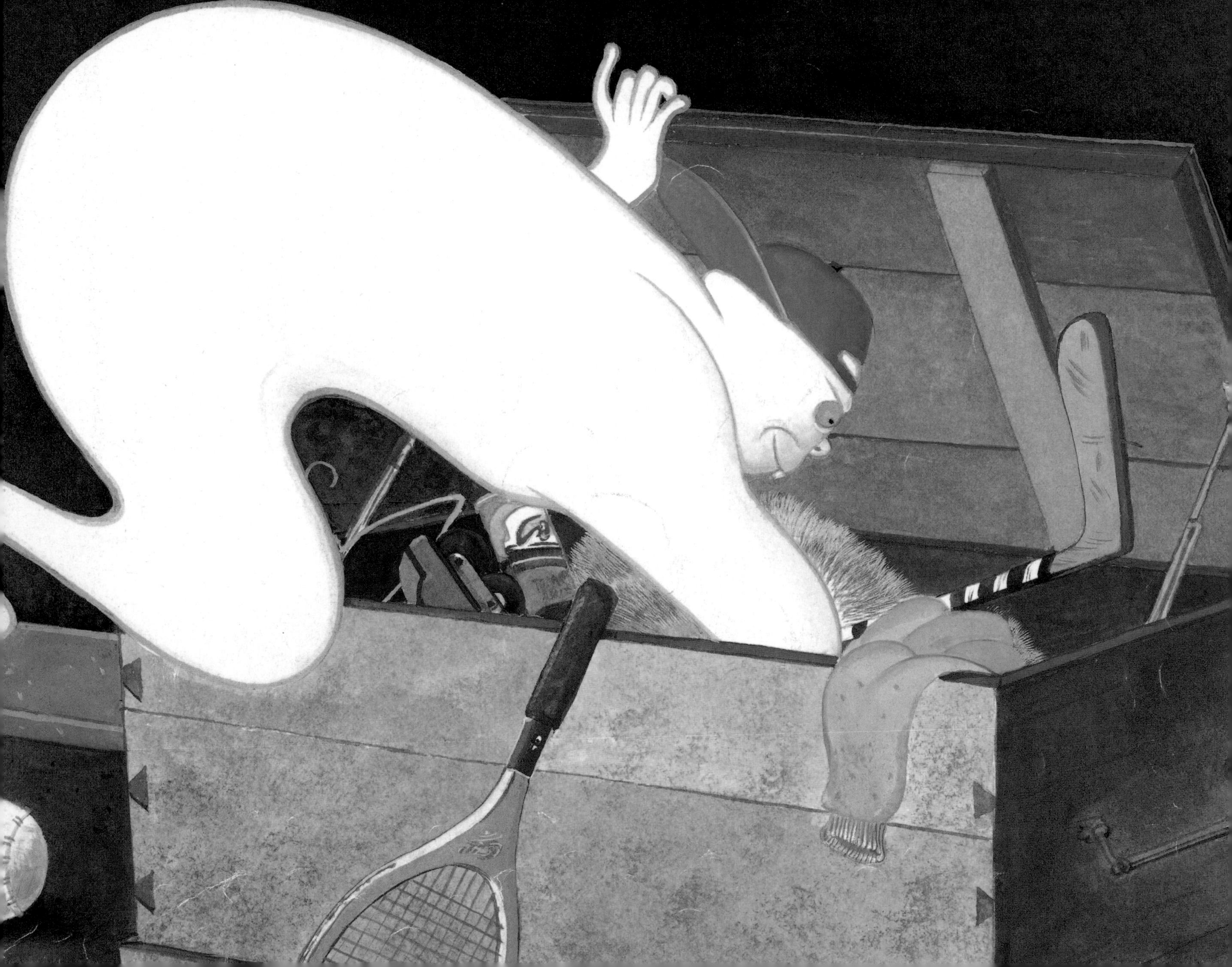

Found a mirror.

hic, hic, hic

Held it up.

hic, hic, hic

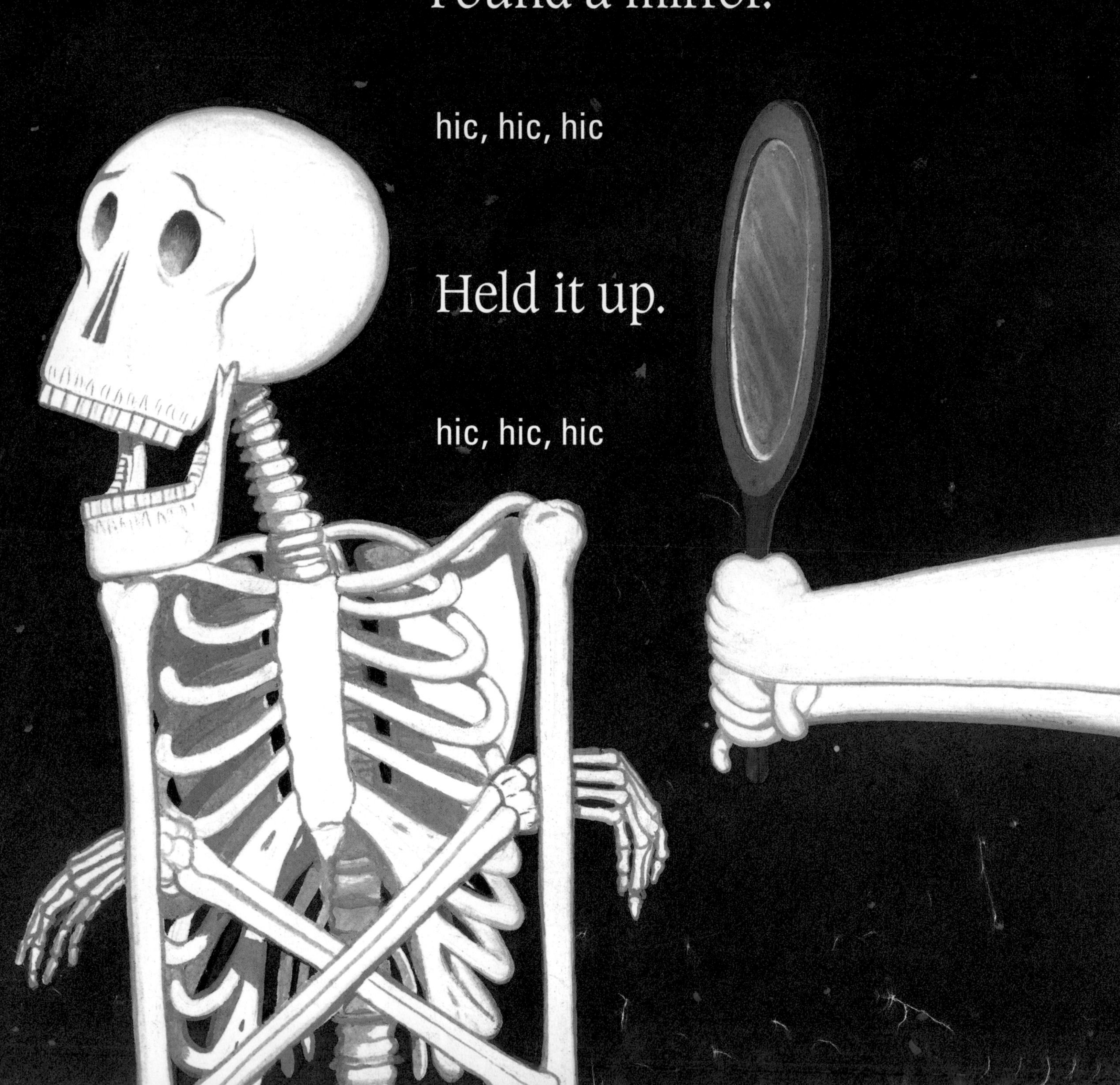

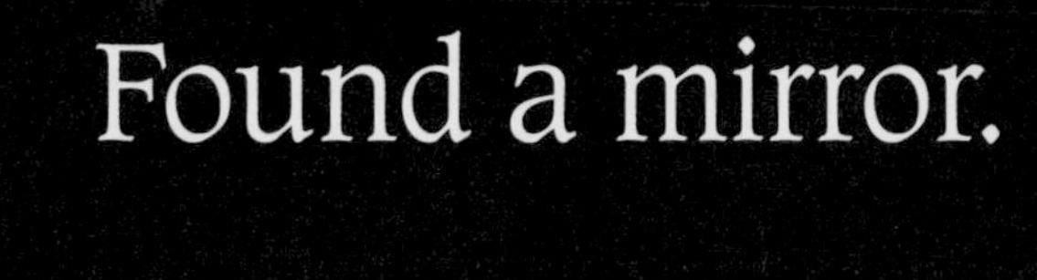

Skeleton screamed!

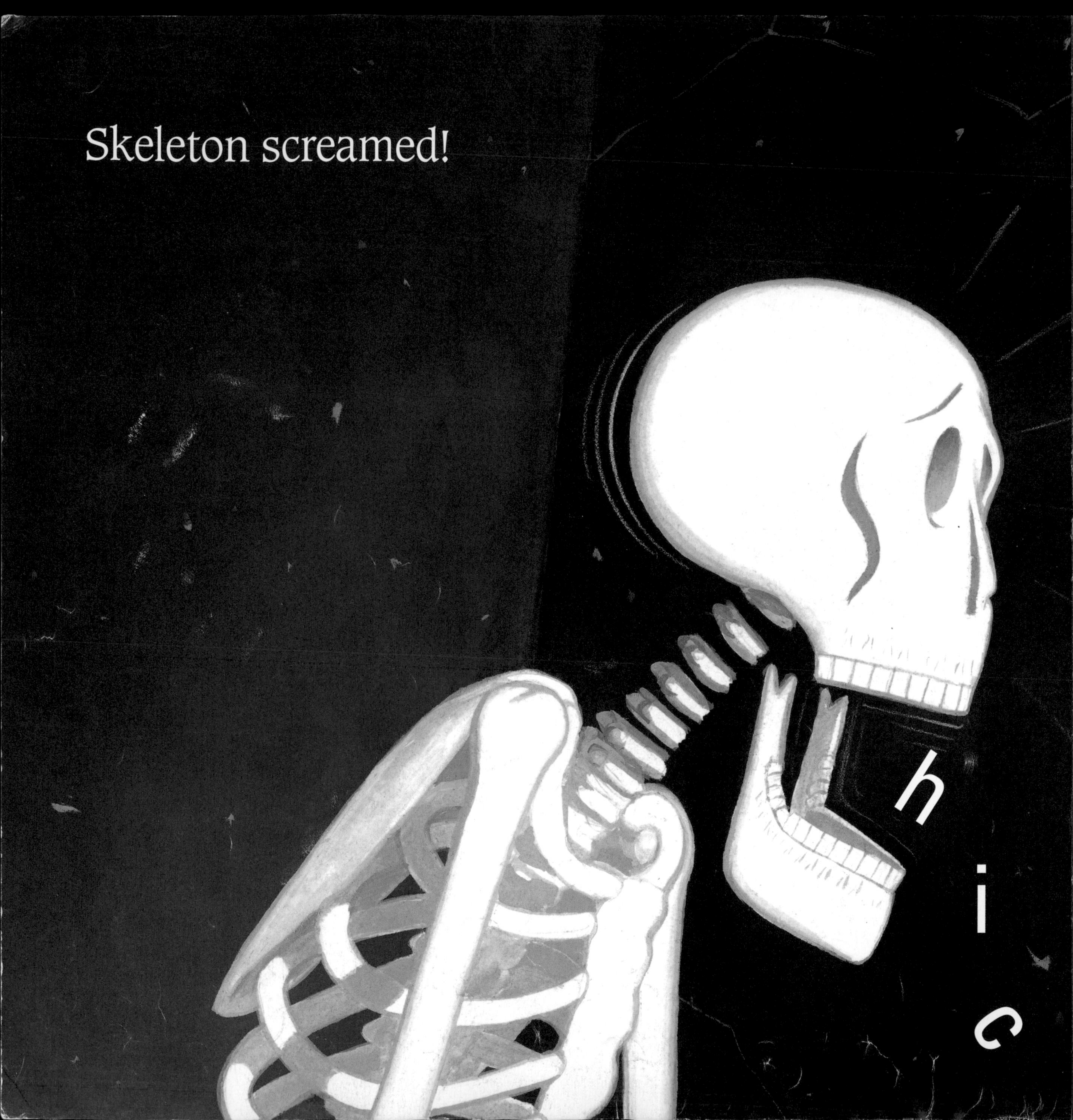

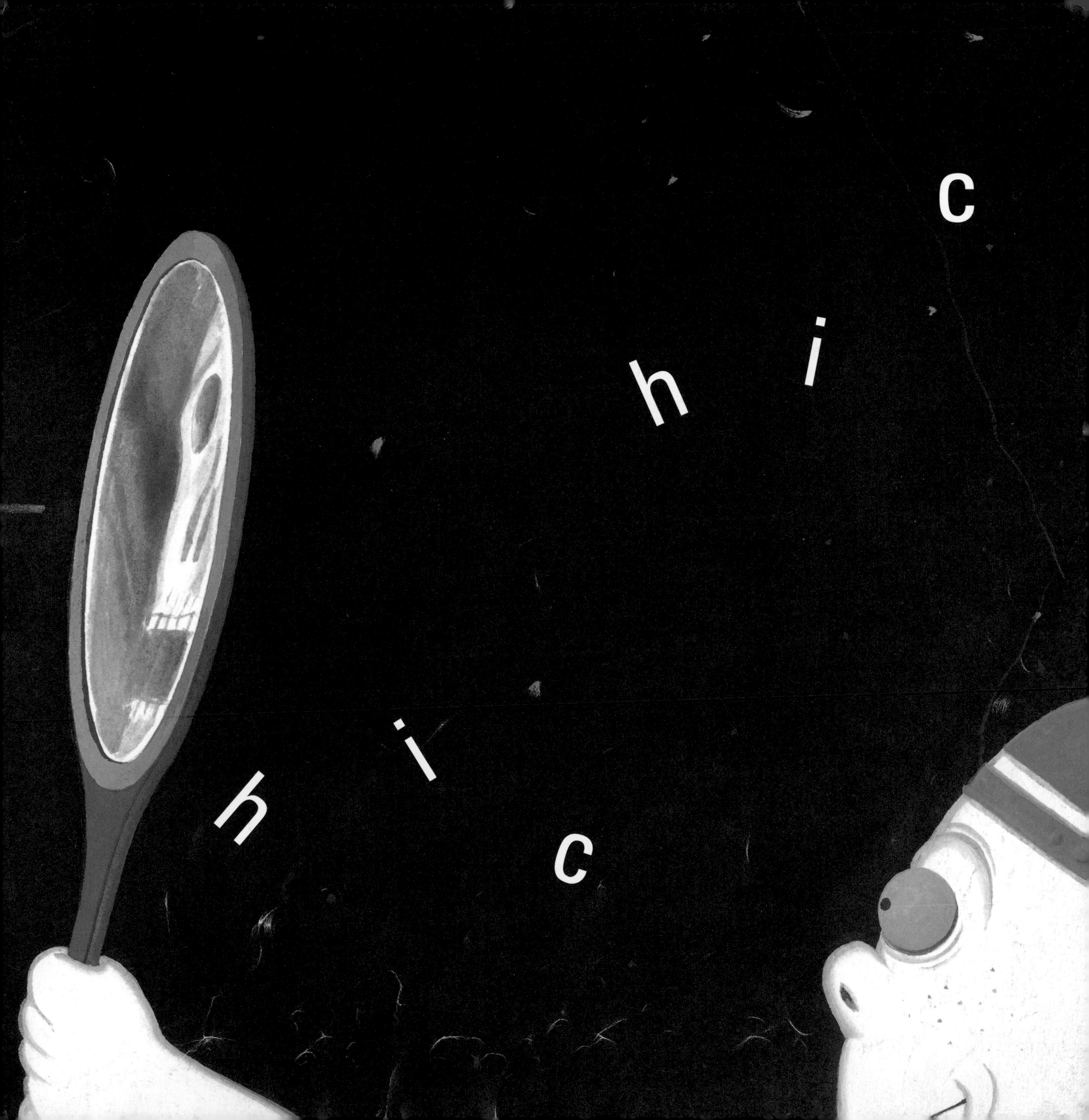
h i c
h i c

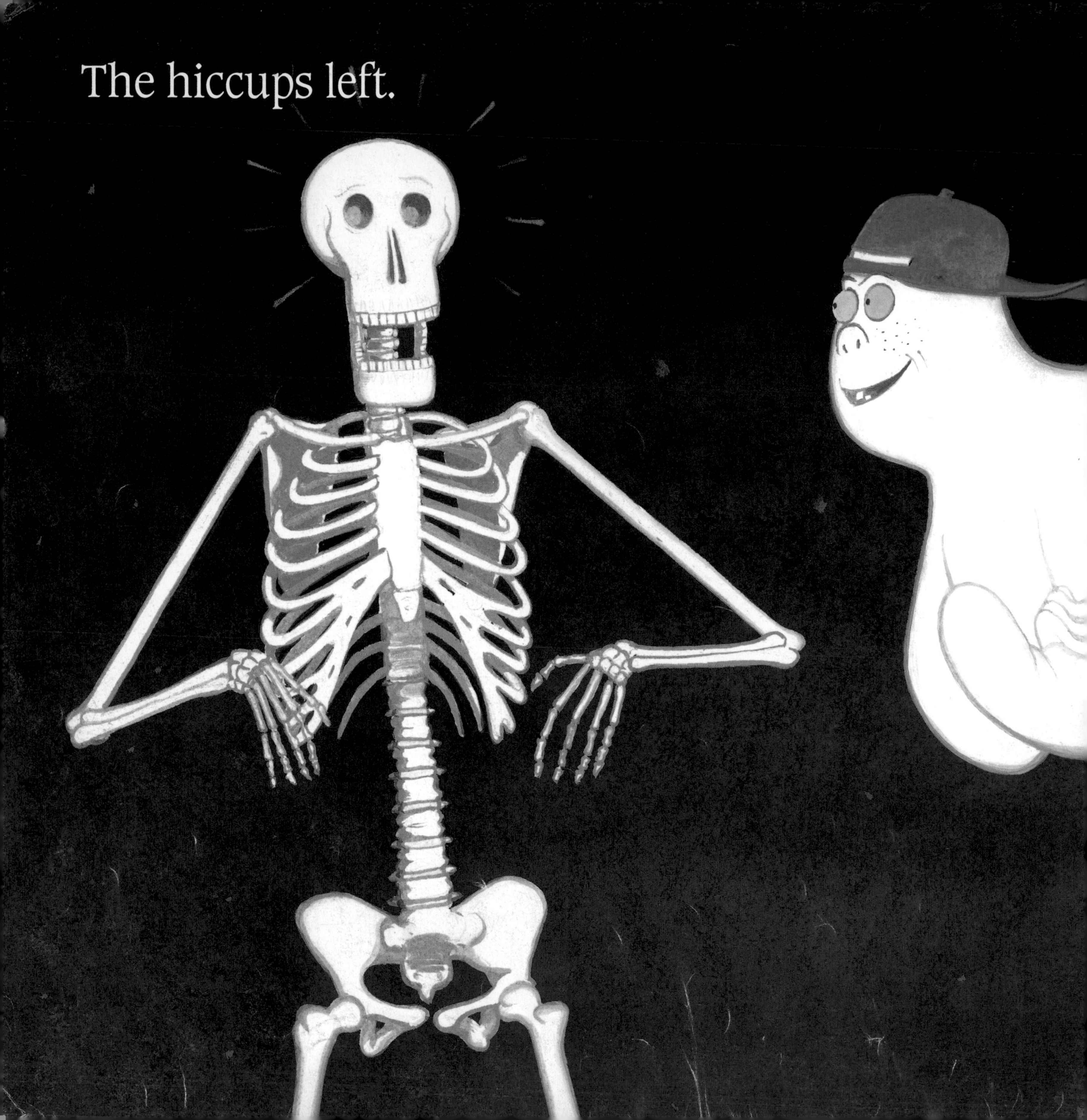
The hiccups left.

hic, hic, hic

They jumped away.
hic,
hic,
hic
Hooray!